SNOWPLOW

BY DENNIS R. SHEALY • ILLUSTRATED BY BOB STAAKE

A GOLDEN BOOK • NEW YORK

Text copyright © 2020 by Dennis R. Shealy
Cover art and interior illustrations copyright © 2020 by Bob Staake
All rights reserved. Published in the United States by Golden Books, an imprint of Random House
Children's Books, a division of Penguin Random House LLC, 1745 Broadway, New York, NY 10019.
Golden Books, A Golden Book, A Little Golden Book, the G colophon, and the distinctive gold
spine are registered trademarks of Penguin Random House LLC.
rhcbooks.com
Educators and librarians, for a variety of teaching tools, visit us at RHTeachersLibrarians.com
Library of Congress Control Number: 2019937139
ISBN 978-0-593-12559-5 (trade) — ISBN 978-0-593-12560-1 (ebook)
Printed in the United States of America
10 9 8 7 6 5 4 3 2

When the temperature drops and snow covers everything in a big blanket of white, I get the call to get goin'. My name is Dusty Bumper, and if you haven't guessed it yet, I'm a

SNOWPLOW!

SNOW ALERT

SALT

When you see me comin',
you know that means snow
is comin', too . . . probably
lots of it!

Clearing snow is an important job, but I have work to do even before the first snowflake falls. I drive through town spreading salt all over the streets. *Why?*

Salt keeps the snow from freezing into ice. And ice can be dangerous if cars, trucks, or *you* slip and slide on it.

I have these little sayings to make sure I'm ready for anything:
    If my tires have traction, I'm ready for *action*!

If my blade's *sharp* and *WIDE*,
I can push the snow aside!

Oh, yeah, I'm all set—and just in time!
Look at all that . . .

I rev my engine and dig in. My blade cuts deep into the snow as I push it out of the way, leaving the road clear.

There are a lot of roads in town, and all of 'em are piled high with snow. I make sure to plow 'em all so the way is clear for ambulances, police cars, and fire trucks.

They're busy keeping people safe, too!

Snow can be fun—especially when there's just enough for a snow day and you get to stay home from school! You can ride sleds, build snowmen, and throw snowballs.

If you like ice-skating, you probably know
my good friend Zamboni. He makes the ice
smooth as glass. And his name is fun to say.
"Hi there, ZAMBONI!"

But too much snow can keep people from getting where they need to go. I've got lots of buddies who push the fluffy stuff out of the way. Shovels and snowblowers are a big help to me and everyone around town.

Big rotary snowplows on the front of trains can move mountains of snow so the trains can go, go, go!

Which reminds me: things that go up must come down. Let's get to the airport, pronto! The runways need to get cleared off before the airplanes can land.

Whew, that was a close one!

Look at all the people and stuff comin' out of those planes. Let's get the people home and the stuff where it needs goin'.

Taxis, buses, and delivery trucks follow me down the highway as I clear a path.

All the roads are plowed, and everyone is back where they belong. There might even be school tomorrow.

I guess I should head home, too.
My job is done. . . .

Oh, no—snow!